SPORTS
in Different Places

Robin Johnson

🌳 Crabtree Publishing Company
www.crabtreebooks.com

Learning About Our
GLOBAL COMMUNITY

Author: Robin Johnson

Publishing plan research and development:
Reagan Miller

Substantive editor: Reagan Miller

Editor: Janine Deschenes

Notes to educators: Janine Deschenes

Proofreader: Ellen Rodger

Design: Samara Parent

Photo research: Robin Johnson & Samara Parent

Production coordinator and prepress technician:
Samara Parent

Print coordinator: Margaret Amy Salter

Photographs:
Alamy: © Ulrich Doering: p13 (top); © Cal Sport Media: p17 (bottom); © Francis Cassidy: p18 (bottom); © martin berry: p19 (bottom)
Bigstock: © jaboardm: cover
Getty: © Junko Kimura: p5 (top), p10; © ERIKA SANTELICES/AFP: p15 (top); © TORSTEN BLACKWOOD: p19 (top)
iStock: © Bildehagen: p4 (top), p16 (bottom); © kali9: p20 (bottom)
Shutterstock: © Lorimer Images: title page, © Paolo Bona: p3 (top); © Tukaram.Karve: p3 (bottom); © hurricanehank: p6 (left), p8 (top); © Tumarkin Igor - ITPS: p7 (bottom); © Aspen Photo: p11 (top); © Grigory Ignatev: p12 (bottom); © Martchan: p13 (bottom); © Anubhab Roy: p14; © A.RICARDO: p21
Wikimedia Commons: © Wisekwai: p18 (top)
All other images by Shutterstock

Front cover: Players compete in a lacrosse game
Title page: A group of Australian lifesavers-in-training compete in a board race.
Contents page: Argentinian soccer fans (upper left); Indian boys playing cricket (lower left)

Library and Archives Canada Cataloguing in Publication

Johnson, Robin (Robin R.), author
    Sports in different places / Robin Johnson.

(Learning about our global community)
Includes index.
Issued in print and electronic formats.
ISBN 978-0-7787-3656-1 (hardcover).--ISBN 978-0-7787-3665-3
(softcover).--ISBN 978-1-4271-1967-4 (HTML)

    1. Sports--Juvenile literature. 2. Games--Juvenile literature.
I. Title.

GV705.4.J64 2017   j796   C2017-905148-2
                                            C2017-905149-0

Library of Congress Cataloging-in-Publication Data

CIP available at the Library of Congress

Crabtree Publishing Company

www.crabtreebooks.com   1-800-387-7650

Printed in the USA/102017/CG20170907

Published in Canada
Crabtree Publishing
616 Welland Ave.
St. Catharines, Ontario
L2M 5V6

Published in the United States
Crabtree Publishing
PMB 59051
350 Fifth Avenue, 59th Floor
New York, New York 10118

Published in the United Kingdom
Crabtree Publishing
Maritime House
Basin Road North, Hove
BN41 1WR

Published in Australia
Crabtree Publishing
3 Charles Street
Coburg North
VIC 3058

Contents

Our Global Community

People all around the world play a role in their **communities**. A community is a group of people who live, work, and play in the same area. Each person belongs to a local community. This includes their home and school. Together, we all belong to one big community—the global community. There are billions of people who live on planet Earth.

cross-country skiing, Norway (page 16)

ARCTIC OCEAN

CANADA

NORTH AMERICA

NORTH PACIFIC OCEAN

U.S.A.

NORTH ATLANTIC OCEAN

MEXICO

ECUADOR

BRAZIL
SOUTH AMERICA

ARGENTINA

lacrosse, Canada (page 11)

Different and alike

People around the world speak, dress, and live in different ways. People also play different sports in different places. Learning about our global community helps us see how we are different and alike in some ways. It helps us learn how we are connected.

In this book, you will learn about sports played in different places around the world. Many of these places are shown on the map below.

ARCTIC OCEAN

ASIA

NORWAY   FINLAND

UNITED KINGDOM

GERMANY

EUROPE

ITALY

SPAIN

CHINA

JAPAN

NORTH PACIFIC OCEAN

PAKISTAN

AFRICA

INDIA

LAOS

THAILAND

ETHIOPIA

MALAYSIA

sumo wrestling, Japan (page 10)

sepak takraw, Laos (page 18)

SOUTH ATLANTIC OCEAN

AUSTRALIA

surfing, Australia (page 19)

What Are Sports?

Sports are active games or **physical** activities. Some sports have rules that players must follow. Players compete against others in the same sport. Sometimes they try to win ribbons, medals, trophies, or other prizes. Other sports are for exercise or fun. What is your favorite sport?

This girl won a medal for horseback riding.

All sorts of sports

There are all sorts of sports! Some sports are team sports. Players work together to beat other teams. Basketball, football, baseball, hockey, and volleyball are some team sports. Other sports are **individual** sports. People play and compete on their own in these sports. Cycling, running, fishing, skiing, swimming, and golf are some individual sports.

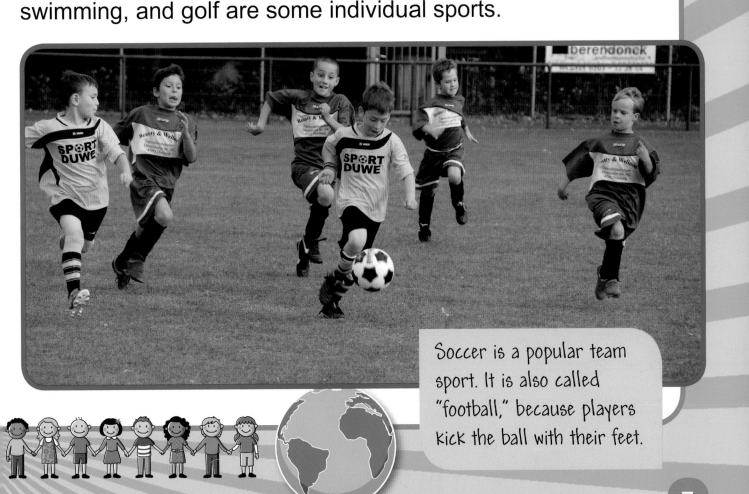

Soccer is a popular team sport. It is also called "football," because players kick the ball with their feet.

A Common Goal

Sports are an important part of communities. Many communities have places where people gather to play sports. Some of these places are outdoors, and others are indoors. People play basketball and tennis on indoor or outdoor courts. They play football and baseball in local parks, swim in pools, and do tricks in skate parks.

Table tennis, or ping-pong, is popular in China. It is played outside in parks and playgrounds, and inside schools across the country.

Sports fans

People in communities also come together to watch sports. Fans are people who cheer for certain players or teams. Some fans cheer for teams in local **leagues**. A league is a group of sports teams that play against one another on a regular basis. Players wear uniforms and have coaches who help them learn skills. Other fans gather to watch **professional** sports teams. The fans meet in huge buildings or outdoor areas to cheer on their favorite players. Go team!

Sports fans often dress in their team colors. Sometimes they even paint their faces or wear silly costumes!

Sports Culture

Sports are often part of a community's **culture**. Culture is a way of life shared by a group of people. It includes their language, clothing, and food. Sumo wrestling is an important part of Japan's culture. It is a sport that has been performed there for more than 1,500 years. In a sumo match, one wrestler tries to force another wrestler off their feet, or out of a circle marked on the ground.

These boys are training to become sumo wrestlers in Japan.

National sports

Some countries have **national sports**. A national sport is an important part of a country's culture and history. It is not always the most popular sport in the country. Lacrosse is Canada's national summer sport. It was invented by **Indigenous** peoples there hundreds of years ago. Lacrosse is a team sport that is played on a field. Players use long sticks to carry, pass, catch, and shoot a hard rubber ball. They earn points by throwing the ball into the other team's net.

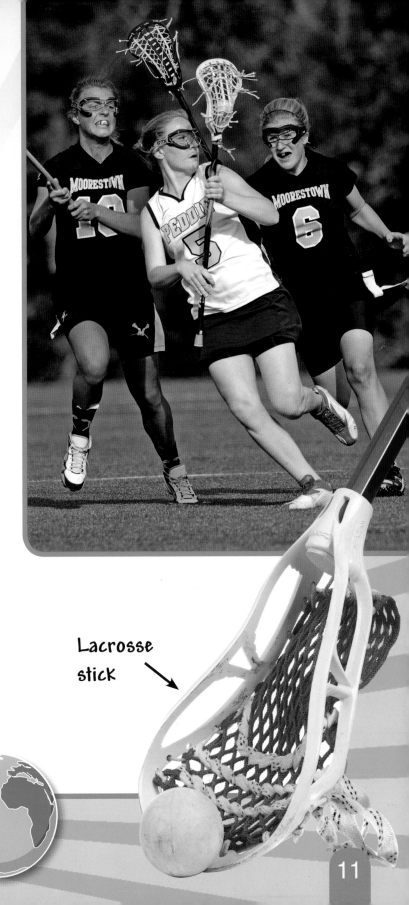

Lacrosse stick

The Beautiful Game

Soccer is the most popular sport in the world. More than 250 million people in 200 countries play it. It is a huge part of the culture in Brazil, Argentina, Spain, England, Germany, Italy, Mexico, and many other places. Players on one soccer team try to get a ball into the other team's net without using their hands.

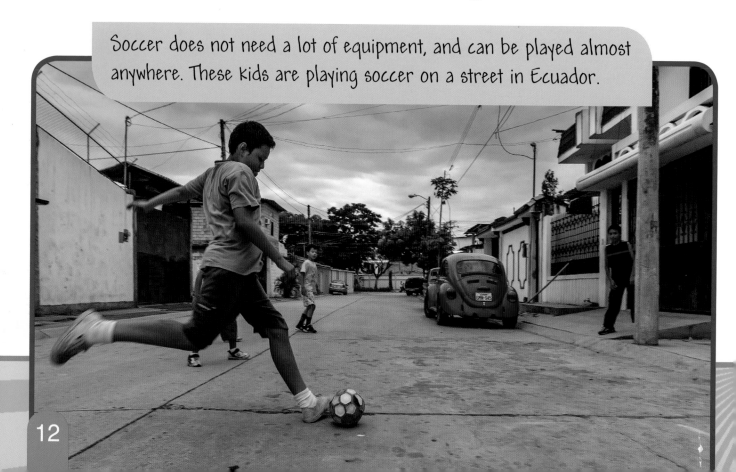

Soccer does not need a lot of equipment, and can be played almost anywhere. These kids are playing soccer on a street in Ecuador.

Make some noise!

People around the world love to watch soccer, too! They gather around their TVs or go to **stadiums** to cheer for their teams. Soccer fans have some noisy **traditions**. A tradition is a way of doing things that is passed down from adults to children. Some fans sing, chant, and beat drums at soccer games. Fans in South Africa blow long horns called *vuvuzelas*. They sound like the loud sounds that elephants make.

vuvuzela

People also play soccer indoors—and on tables! These boys in Ethiopia are playing a table soccer game called foosball.

Bats and Balls

Many sports are played with bats and balls. Players may throw, catch, hit, or kick the balls, depending on the sport. Many people in countries such as India, Pakistan, and Australia are crazy about cricket! This sport is played on a field with wooden stumps called wickets at each end. A player from one team throws a ball toward a wicket and tries to knock it down. A player from the other team tries to hit the ball away from the wicket and into the field to score runs.

Cricket players use a flat wooden bat to hit the ball.

wicket

Baseball is the national sport of the Dominican Republic.

Batter up!

Baseball is popular in the United States. It is called America's **pastime**. Baseball is a team sport that is played outdoors on a field. A player on one team uses a rounded bat to hit a ball thrown by a player on the other team. After they hit the ball, the batter runs around the field and touches four bases on the ground. If they touch all four, they earn a run. The other team catches the ball and throws it to a base to get the runner out.

It is a tradition for fans to eat hot dogs and peanuts at baseball games.

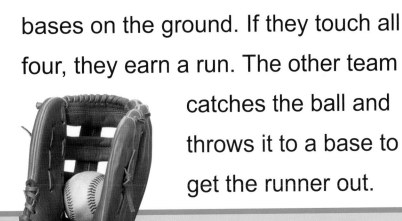

15

Cold Climates

Different parts of the world have different **climates**. Climate is the usual weather in an area. Climates can be cold or hot, and wet or dry. Sports such as skiing, skating, and ice hockey are popular in places with cold climates. Norway and Finland have long, cold winters. The ground is covered with ice and snow for months. People there used to cross-country ski to travel the long distances between communities.

cross-country skis

Cross-country skiing is the national sport of Norway.

On the ice

Ice hockey is a team sport that can only be played on ice. It is very popular in Canada and is the country's national winter sport. Canada has cold, icy winters. People there play hockey outdoors on frozen ponds and ice **rinks**. They also play hockey indoors in **arenas**. Players wear skates on their feet to glide on the ice. They use sticks to shoot rubber discs called pucks into nets.

It is a tradition for fans to throw their hats on the ice if a hockey player scores a hat trick, or three goals in one game.

Warm Weather

Some parts of the world have warm climates. The weather is hot and sunny all year round. People cannot go skiing or ice skating outdoors there! Countries such as Thailand, Malaysia, and Laos have warm climates. Children there can play outdoor sports, such as *sepak takraw*, all year. Sepak takraw is a team sport. It is also called kick volleyball. Players try to get a ball over a net without using their hands.

rattan ball

These children in Laos are playing sepak takraw. The ball is often made of **rattan**, the stems of a type of palm tree.

Water world

Some places with warm climates are found near bodies of water. People who live near the water can go swimming, surfing, or sailing all year. These water sports are popular in Australia. It is an island with a warm climate. There are many sandy beaches there. Australians often spend holidays playing sports at the beach.

Even Santa Claus goes to the beach on Christmas in Australia!

These girls are competing in a surfing contest in Australia. They will stand on their boards and ride the ocean waves.

Wide World of Sports

Sports are fun for everyone! People of all ages, sizes, skills, and **abilities** can play sports. Some people who have **intellectual** disabilities take part in a series of sports contests called the Special Olympics. To have a disability means to have a **limited** ability to do something. Athletes train and compete in bowling, swimming, skating, gymnastics, and other sports.

Nearly five million athletes take part in the Special Olympics. It is held in 172 countries around the world.

More than 100,000 people play wheelchair basketball around the world. These basketball players are competing at the 2016 Paralympic Games.

Global Games

The best athletes in the world can compete for their countries. Some try to win medals at the **Olympic Games** or **Paralympic Games**. The Olympic Games are a series of sports contests for the world's top athletes. The Paralympics are sports contests for the best athletes with physical disabilities. These events take place in a different country every four years. They bring athletes and fans together from all around the world.

Notes to Educators

Objective:

This title encourages readers to make global connections by understanding that even though people around the world play different sports, most people gather in their communities to play or watch group and individual sports, and sports often have similar characteristics.

Main Concepts Include:

- Sports can bring communities together.
- Sports may differ from one another, but they often have similar characteristics such as equipment, goals, and players.

Discussion Prompts:

- Revisit the types of sports from around the world described in the book. Connect each sport to the climate or environment in which it is played. Ask readers how each sport is suited for the climate or environment. How does each sport compare to the sports they play or watch? How are they the same and different?

Activity Suggestions:

- Invite children to explore a sport that is played in the global community. Encourage them to write down as much information as possible. Provide sentence starters such as:
  - _____ is an individual/team sport.
  - This sport uses this equipment: _____, _____, _____.
  - This sport is played in a _____ climate/environment.
- Ask children to consider how the same sport might be played in their local community. Or, if their chosen sport is already played in their community, how might it be played in a community in another part of the world. How might the teams, equipment, location, or rules be modified to fit the characteristics of a new community?
- Invite students to create a Venn Diagram, chart, or list to compare how the same sport might be played in two different communities.
- Encourage children to point out how the climate or environment changes and how the sport is played.

22

Learning More

Books

Haw, Jennie. *Score! The Story of Soccer.* Crabtree Publishing, 2014.

Lewis, Clare. *Games Around the World.* Heinemann, 2014.

Ward, Leslie. *Players Around the World.* Teacher Created Materials, 2017.

Websites

www.sikids.com
Visit the Sports Illustrated Kids website for news, photos, games, and more.

www.specialolympics.org/
Visit this website to learn more about the Special Olympics.

www.littlepassports.com/blog/world-community/after-school-sports-around-the-world/
Find out which sports kids play after school all around the world.

Glossary

Note: Some **boldfaced** words are defined where they appear in the book.

ability [uh-BIL-i-tee] (noun) The skill, means, or capacity to do something

arena [uh-REE-nuh] (noun) An area where events are held, surrounded by seats

Indigenous [In-DIJ-en-ous] (adjective) Living naturally in, or native to a place

individual [in-duh-VIJ-oo-uh l] (adjective) Played or done by one person

intellectual [in-tl-EK-choo-uh l] (adjective) Relating to one's intellect, or mind

limited [LIM-i-tid] (adjective) Restricted, or not in a large amount

pastime [PAS-tahym] (noun) A hobby or activity done for fun

physical [FIZ-i-kuh l] (adjective) About or done by a person's body

professional [pruh-FESH-uh-nl] (adjective) Doing a sport or other activity as a job

rink [ringk] (noun) A smooth area of ice made for skating

stadium [STEY-dee-uh m] (noun) A large, open structure with rows of seats all around

A noun is a person, place, or thing. An adjective tells us what something is like.

Index